BATTLE WITH THE WITHER

AN UNOFFICIAL OVERWORLD ADVENTURE, BOOK SIX

BATTLE WITH THE WITHER

DANICA DAVIDSON

Sky Pony Press
New York

Sky Pony Press books may be purchased in bulk at special discounts for sales
promotion, corporate gifts, fund-raising, or educational purposes. Special
editions can also be created to specifications. For details, contact the Special
Sales Department, Sky Pony Press, 307 West 36th Street, 11th Floor, New
York, NY 10018 or info@skyhorsepublishing.com.

Visit our website at www.skyponypress.com.

10 9 8 7 6 5 4 3 2 1

Library of Congress Cataloging-in-Publication Data is available on file.

Cover illustration by Lordwhitebear
Cover design by Brian Peterson

*Special thanks to James Fitzgerald, Krishan Trotman and Rachel Stark, Jeremy
Bonebreak, Dalton, Tobias and Rin, Eileen Robinson, Dan Woren, Alexis
Tirado, Caitlin Abber, Deborah Peckham and Peter Davidson, and Taylor Hite.*

Box Set IBSN: 978-1-5107-1533-2
Ebook ISBN: 978-1-5107-1623-0

Printed in China

BATTLE WITH THE WITHER

CHAPTER 1

"**I** THINK THERE'S A MONSTER NEARBY," I SAID, FEELing a chill.

Dad and I both looked out the window at the sunny day. Monsters only came out after dark in the Overworld, but knowing this didn't make me feel any better. I felt a terrible sense of dread in my stomach; it kept telling me danger was coming closer.

"You're just jumpy because of Herobrine," Dad said gruffly.

He had a point. Last week my cousin Alex and my friends from Earth, Maison, Destiny, and Yancy and I had all defeated Herobrine in a world-spanning battle that had brought us to the End and back. That would put anyone on edge.

Dad continued talking to me, but I wasn't listening. It wasn't that I was *trying* to ignore him. It's just that I knew something bad was going to happen, the same way I had known it in my gut when Herobrine was first rising to power—back before I had even known that Herobrine existed.

So I was staring out the window at the cloudless sky, squinting my eyes and looking for some unnatural zombie that could attack during daylight hours, or a rampaging giant spider that had gone hostile. Instead I just saw grass and flowers and trees—everything was the way it should be. And then I saw Dad's angry face right in front of me.

"Stevie!" he said, blocking the window. "You haven't been listening to a word I've said."

Caught, I put my head down and sighed. "I'm sorry."

Dad huffed.

Dad had decided that today was going to be a "father-son" day, though I didn't really know what that meant. Earlier I'd tried to go to my special portal to Earth so I could visit Maison, Destiny, and Yancy in their world. But before I could step out the door, Dad had appeared in front of me with a Where-Do-You-Think-You're-Going? look.

When I'd tried to explain, he had said, "All you've done lately is hang out with your Earth friends. It's time we spent a day together."

But so far all we'd done was sit at the table while Dad told stories about the monsters he'd slain when he was younger. He was reminding me about how he'd made his diamond sword when he was twelve, which used to intimidate me a few months ago when all I had ever made was a wooden sword. That wooden sword had been broken, but it was still hanging on the wall because I'd broken it in the first real fight Dad had seen me in. He'd been impressed by my fighting skills, though it was hard for him to say that.

"If you were listening," Dad was telling me now, "you would have heard me talk about the importance of always bringing along a Potion of Healing when you go on a mission against mobs."

"Mobs" was what we people in the Overworld sometimes called the monsters that lived all around us.

"Potion of Healing, yeah, got it," I said, trying to peek around him out the window. What was that movement I saw out there? Was it something dangerous? The thing moved once more and I saw it was just a chicken.

"Stevie!" Dad said again. I tore my eyes away from the window and trained them back on his face. He continued, "I'm serious about the Potion of Healing. In these past few months, you've stopped a zombie attack on a school, thwarted a zombie takeover of the Overworld, and beaten Herobrine. But that doesn't mean you're invincible. You could still get hurt."

Of course I knew I could still get hurt. That's why I was so worried about this sense of dread I had.

Still, I could tell Dad was getting more and more annoyed with me, so I sat back at the table and made myself stop peeking out the window. Some father-son day this was turning out to be. I wondered what Maison and the others were up to. If they were here, I bet they'd go exploring with me, and we could figure out what was making me so anxious.

"Stevie," Dad said, a little more gently this time. He wasn't good at talking in a gentle way, because he was more of a gruff, Take-It-Or-Leave-It kind of guy. In some ways we weren't alike at all, which was weird, because he was my own family. Weren't fathers and sons supposed to be more similar than we were?

"It feels as if we haven't spent any time together lately," he went on. "I just want to give you the knowledge I have of the Overworld to protect you."

I knew he meant well. The problem was that Dad's talks had a tendency to turn into lectures . . . which turned into me having my mind wander.

"I just keep feeling like I'm forgetting something," I said. Ossie, our cat, had come into the room and jumped up on the windowsill, as if she also felt a need to keep a lookout. "Something important."

Dad looked annoyed, as if he thought I was making stuff up as an excuse for not listening. "It's broad daylight and we're in a well-built house. There is absolutely nothing to worry abo—"

He stopped when the whole sky went red like an evil shadow was dropping. A wailing rose up. One of the cries sounded like the weeping of ghasts, but how could that be? Ghasts didn't live in the Overworld! I realized I was hearing the sounds of many different monsters, all of them crying out.

"Impossible!" Dad said. I had already jumped to my feet and raced to the window.

"No!" I gasped when I saw it.

CHAPTER 2

OSSIE HISSED AT WHAT SHE SAW AND LEAPT DOWN from the window, but Dad and I could only stand there and stare in shock. The sunny sky I'd looked at moments before was gone. Outside my window was a world of flame and lava, as if the Nether had taken over the Overworld.

The sky had turned a dark red, mimicking the ceiling of the Nether and giving the whole landscape a creepy, reddish haze. Spots of fire dotted our farmland, and the little creek in the distance had gone orange-red with sputters of lava.

I thought my eyes had to be fooling me, but the red sky, fire, and lava weren't the only Nether-like things out there—there were also Nether mobs! I could see an army of zombie pigmen, all of them holding golden swords. They were squealing and charging among themselves. A pair of ghasts flew overhead, screaming out their hideous cries, noises that shook me to the core.

And were those wither skeletons I saw in the distance, hulking tall and angry-looking against the red sky?

I stared beyond the wither skeletons, and what I saw was even worse. It was a huge Nether fortress with jagged edges like a mountain, looking as if it had been built out of darkness. There was no way anyone would have had time to build that between now and the last time I had peeked out the window. What was going on here?

Dad had grabbed his diamond sword, which was his prized possession. He looked ready to fight. I wasn't so sure, though. How would you even go about fighting a whole Nether landscape? Nothing like this had ever happened in the Overworld, because the fiery realm of the Nether had always been a separate place!

"What if it stays like this?" I asked in a low voice. After journeying with my cousin Alex through the Nether once, not long ago, I'd promised myself never to visit there again. And now here the Nether was, right on my doorstep!

"It seems to be this way as far as I can see," Dad said, squinting out the window. "I'm going to the village to investigate and make sure the people there are safe."

"What if this is affecting Earth too?" I asked. "I have to find Maison—"

Dad grabbed me before I could run off. "You're staying right here in the Overworld!" he said.

I was shocked. Dad had always taught me the importance of helping others. How come he could go check on the villagers, but he didn't like the idea of me checking on *my* friends?

"You're completely obsessed with that portal," Dad said. "That's all you talk about anymore. Maison, the portal, Earth, the portal. I'm surprised you're ever in the Overworld these days. All you do is go back and forth to Earth."

"That's not true," I said. "I went to the Nether, remember? You broke down the portal afterward."

Dad looked at me, confused. For a moment there was a terrible silence between us. All I could hear was the sound of ghasts crying outside our door.

"What portal?" Dad asked.

"The one to the Nether that Alex and I built next to the house," I said. "We were in such a rush to defeat Herobrine that we didn't break it right away, but when I came back home it was gone, so I figured you destroyed it."

"I never saw any portal," Dad said. "I definitely never broke one next to the house."

Something clicked in my brain, and I think my face went as red as the sky outside. Then my face must have gone skeleton-white as I realized what this meant. The Nether portal—that's what I'd been forgetting!

"Do you think . . . that the missing portal to the Nether might have to do with what's going on?" I asked. I couldn't connect the dots, yet somehow I also couldn't stop from feeling that these two things were related.

"Portals don't go missing," Dad said. "If neither of us broke that portal, someone else must have. Besides, even though some mobs can get out of a Nether portal and come into the Overworld, it wouldn't explain all of this."

"Well, the Nether mobs shouldn't have been able to follow us out of that portal, anyway," I said quickly, trying to make things sound a little better. But my sense of dread was getting worse. I had a feeling I'd really blown it this time. "Because a Wither showed up just as we were leaving the Nether and blew up the area around the portal."

It had been quite a sight. I'd never seen a Wither before—they were legendary. Withers had three black skeleton heads and could fly through the air, shooting skulls out of their three mouths. The one we'd seen was bigger than a house.

This caught Dad's attention. "A Wither? But who created it?"

I stared at him blankly. "I don't know. As far as I could tell, there was no one else around." I didn't want to add that we had been fleeing a group of angry zombie pigmen that *I* had accidentally made angry. So even if there had been other people around when that Wither showed up, I probably wouldn't have noticed them.

"Withers need to be created by humans using soul sand and wither skulls," Dad said. "They don't spawn naturally like other mobs. Someone had to have created that Wither you saw. And Withers are no joke, Stevie—the destruction they cause is beyond belief."

Before I could say anything more, I heard a strange whistling, like an approaching storm. And then a roaring. Dad and I both looked at each other for a moment, wide-eyed.

The next thing I knew, the wall of our house had been blasted out, sending us flying.

CHAPTER 3

I HIT THE GROUND, GRUNTING AS A BOOKSHELF TOP-pled over and a landslide of books fell on me. As soon as I pushed the books off, my vision was filled with nothing but the dark red sky and the blurring, raging image of an enormous Wither.

The Wither whirled overhead, easily breaking up the entire side wall of our house, as if it were made of eggshells. The three-headed creature was spitting out skulls in all directions, the skulls landing and exploding like TNT. In an instant Dad's supply shed next to the house was gone; in the next, half our living room was on fire.

Dad was nowhere to be seen, so he must be buried under the all the fallen debris. A rush of panic ran up my throat as I realized I was going to have to stop the Wither myself before I could find Dad and make sure he was okay.

"Get out of my home!" I yelled, as if the Wither could understand.

To my surprise, the Wither turned its six white-line eyes to me, as if it did hear and understand. But it definitely didn't stop the attack.

I scrambled out of the debris, trying to find my diamond sword. Where was it? My shaky hands hunted through the rubble and I finally grabbed a block that had once been a part of our wall. It would have to work as a weapon.

I charged at the Wither, and the giant monster spun out of the way, still hurling skulls in all directions. Our house was getting more and more damaged by the second. Dad had spent years building this house!

Just as I was about to reach the Wither, it opened its mouth and a skull came rushing straight toward me! I wouldn't have been able to get out of the way in time, but Dad appeared out of nowhere and pushed me aside. The skull landed right where I had been, blowing a hole into the ground.

"Dad!" I cried, relieved to see he was okay. And if he hadn't gotten out of the debris and pushed me out of the way in time, I wouldn't still be here!

"I am Steve, the feared mob slayer," Dad shouted at the Wither. "Stay away from my son!"

Dad quickly hoisted himself on top of the fireplace so he could get up higher. Then he launched himself at the Wither, his sword poised high. He slashed the head on the left, barely causing any damage at all, even though it was a direct hit.

I realized I was just standing there, staring in shock, which wasn't helping Dad at all. When he'd pushed me to the side and saved me, I'd dropped my block. Argh, where was my diamond sword? A skull landed right by where Ossie was hiding to the side and she scuttled away, barely escaping.

"Stevie, look out!" Dad cried.

I lunged to the side, rolling myself up in a ball. When I lowered my arms a moment later, I saw that the space where I'd been standing was now completely blasted out. I'd been so consumed with the search for my sword that if Dad hadn't said something, I wouldn't have gotten out of the way in time. That was the second time he'd saved me today.

Dad looked even angrier. Destroying his house was one thing, but when he saw the Wither almost take out Ossie and me, I saw Dad reach a level of anger I didn't know was possible for him. He hurled himself at the middle head of the Wither, his sword glimmering, shouting out a battle cry as he attacked.

The Wither turned to him and opened the mouth in its middle head. It didn't shoot him with a skull. By comparison, that might have been the kinder thing to do, because Dad could have taken a Potion of Healing and been all better. Instead, the Wither grabbed the sword in its mouth and bit down on it like it was hungry for dinner.

There was a fearful crunch, and Dad's treasured diamond sword broke into pieces that fell to the ground like rain. There was no way that sword could ever be repaired.

Dad stumbled back, face pale, startled to suddenly find himself without a weapon. The Wither knocked against him, sending him flying against a still-standing wall of the house. Dad groaned on the impact and fell, more debris tumbling on top of him.

My eyes caught sight of something. It was my old, broken wooden sword! It was nothing compared to my diamond sword, but it was within reach, and it wasn't as badly broken as Dad's sword.

I snatched up the broken wooden sword and charged toward the Wither, yelling as if to scare it off. Dad turned to look at me. The Wither turned to look at me. And when the Wither saw what I was holding for self-defense, all three of its heads burst out laughing.

CHAPTER 4

I SKIDDED TO A HALT, STUNNED. WITHERS COULDN'T laugh!

"Oh—oh—you mean to fight me with that!" the middle head shrieked with laughter.

"I told you this was the wrong house," said the left head.

"We're looking for the boy that Herobrine told us about—the one with the portal," said the right head. "But you couldn't possibly be him. Look at you!"

If Withers couldn't laugh, they definitely couldn't talk!

"Herobrine?" I stammered. Just the sound of his name was enough to make me feel sick.

And then I saw something. The Wither was holding on to a Nether portal by the stem of its body. No, not *a* Nether portal. *The* Nether portal Alex and I had made. As I watched, zombie pigmen jumped out of the portal one at a time, landing in the wreckage of our house and milling around.

"You're—you're the Wither I saw in the Nether!" I said. I don't know why I said that. When a Wither breaks down your house out of nowhere, then starts talking and mentions Herobrine, there really isn't any logical thing to say.

"Yes," the middle head replied with a snakelike hiss. "We saw you and a redheaded girl running, not long after Herobrine created us. Herobrine said . . ." The Wither dipped lower as if to share a secret. I automatically jumped back. "That there was a boy with a portal, a portal to a world unlike the Overworld or the Nether," it went on. "And Herobrine said he was going to steal this portal and destroy this boy."

"But Herobrine also said that if anything happened to him," the right head said, "we were created to complete his mission of destruction."

"We felt it when Herobrine was defeated in the End," the left head said. "It was as if a shudder went through the worlds. Then we knew it was our time to shine."

Dad pushed the debris out of his way and slowly dragged himself to his feet, holding his side. He was weakened, although not badly hurt.

"The boy you want isn't here!" Dad shouted, stumbling forward. "Leave!"

The next thing I knew, the middle head popped so close to my face that I thought it would take a bite out of me. "Do you know where the boy we're looking for is?"

I shook my head.

"It doesn't matter," the middle head said. "He can't be far. In the meantime, we're enjoying this Nether portal. Using the power Herobrine gave us, we've made this an extra special portal—one that brings the Nether with us wherever we go."

"I want the boy!" snarled the right head. "Herobrine let him get away, but we won't!"

"We'll find the boy if you just listen to me," snapped the left head. "All we need to do is keep up the Nether attack and find that portal so we can send monsters out through it to that other world. Then we just sit back and enjoy—the rest will take care of itself."

"The boy you're looking for is long gone," Dad said, leaning on his crafting table to support his weight. "So is the portal you're looking for. Go back to the Nether and leave us in peace!"

All three Wither heads laughed at him. "I don't know what's funnier," the middle head declared. "The father who acts tough but loses his sword instantly, or the little boy who tries to be heroic and only has a broken sword. Come on, let's find more fun elsewhere."

The Wither lifted itself out of our broken house, whirling, the Nether portal still in its clutches. As it flew away, hurling skulls, more mobs continued to fall out of the portal.

CHAPTER 5

I RAN TO DAD'S SIDE. NOW I COULD SEE THAT HE WAS in more pain than I realized, and he'd been trying to hide it from the Wither.

"Get a Potion of Healing," Dad gasped, clutching his side, his face streaked with sweat.

Ossie came out from where she was hiding, thankfully unharmed. Frantic, I ran to Dad's supply shed—or where Dad's supply shed used to be. Dad had been collecting materials in that shed for years, since long before I was born, and it had held just about any item you could think of.

But now everything there had either been destroyed or cast about. I dug through piles of smashed potion bottles until I found two Potions of Healing that were intact.

"Here, Dad!" I said, running it over to him. He swigged the drink and almost immediately I could see he felt better.

"I'm sorry, Dad," I said. "I couldn't find my diamond sword."

However, that wasn't the worst thing I was feeling sorry about. I couldn't believe I'd just assumed Dad had broken the portal to the Nether and I'd never looked into it. I should have been more responsible, and now look what had happened! No lecture from Dad could make me feel worse than I already felt, and I think he knew that.

Dad didn't say anything for a moment. He was staring intensely at the broken pieces of his diamond sword, glittering in the dark red light. Then he said, "Find what supplies you can from the shed. We have to warn the villagers."

My heart skipped a beat. That wasn't the only thing I thought we had to do. "We also have to go to the Earth portal and warn Maison!" I said.

Dad gave me a cold look for some reason. "The Wither doesn't know where the Earth portal is. The villagers are in much more immediate danger."

I honestly didn't know *who* was in the most danger right then. Even if the Wither didn't know it, the Earth portal wasn't far from here. I kept it locked up in an obsidian house that most mobs wouldn't be able to break through, but a Wither wasn't like most mobs. I knew the Wither could stumble across the little house and the Earth portal very easily if it kept flying around in this area.

"But, Dad!" I said. "Maison and the others can help us!"

"I said no, Stevie!" Dad said, and this time I got quiet. Dad watched me for a long moment, and then began sifting through things himself. He found his diamond pickaxe and dropped it into his toolkit, along with a few other supplies.

Unsure what to do, I started digging as well. Ossie nudged at something and when I lifted it, there was my diamond sword underneath. I found my tool kit nearby, and I stuck the remaining Potion of Healing into it, in case we needed it later. As I fumbled and put more things into my tool kit, I realized I was still shaking from the attack. Only half my brain was paying attention to what weapons and supplies I dropped in.

The Wither was after me! It wanted to destroy me! But it had looked in my face and laughed at me, thinking I was some dumb kid and not the "boy with the portal" it was after.

I guessed I wasn't much to look at just then. I didn't have a real weapon, and people had judged me before because I was eleven and they thought I couldn't do anything. It hurt but, in a way, it was also good that the Wither had thought I was someone else and spared me.

Dad surveyed the reddish landscape. "I see ghasts, blazes, and magma cubes, but they're all far off," he said. He looked at the zombie pigmen wandering through our skeleton of a house, acting as if they owned the place. I could tell Dad wanted to push them out, but zombie pigmen only left you alone if you left them alone. If Dad got aggressive with one, they'd all attack, which was something I'd learned the hard way during my trip through the Nether. To make matters worse, there were hundreds of zombie pigmen around the farmland that could become enemy attackers in an instant.

"Let's go," Dad said. "Bring the cat so she'll be safe with us."

Not knowing what else to do, I picked up Ossie and trotted after Dad.

"When we get to the village, we'll get the villagers armed and all go after that Wither together," Dad was saying, making plans as he ran.

If the Wither hasn't already ransacked the village, I thought, but didn't say it out loud. I wanted so badly to run to the Earth portal and check on Maison to make sure she was safe!

When we came up to the tree house Maison and I had built, I couldn't take it anymore. Half the tree house was torn down, and the nearby lake had turned from cool blue water into a cesspool of Nether lava. I looked at the boiling lava, and I looked at my tree house, remembering all the good times I had had, hanging out with Maison there. It was our special place.

"I need to go tell Maison!" I blurted, and started running in the direction of the portal. "I'm sorry, but I can't let something happen to her!"

Dad called my name, but I kept running. I agreed with Dad that we needed to get to the villagers to warn them and have them join us in the fight against the Wither. Still, the villagers had fought mobs before.

They had had training. Most people on Earth wouldn't know what to do with a Wither if it burst in on them, let alone if it brought all these Nether mobs with it. The Earth portal wasn't far from here, so I could just run over there, get Maison, have her let the others know what was going on in case anything happened, and then she, Dad, and I would run to the village. It wouldn't be that far out of our way, and it might help save a whole world.

Dad chased after me. Maybe the Potion of Healing hadn't made him a hundred percent better since his fall, because he didn't catch up to me until I was almost at the portal. I felt a rush of relief when I saw the obsidian house was still there, all in one piece. That meant the portal was safe. The land here was also reddish and dotted with fires like the Nether, though I didn't see any Wither-caused destruction.

Then Dad grabbed me and whirled me around to look at him.

"Stevie!" he exclaimed right in my face, gripping me by my shoulders. He looked very emotional, which startled me. "I don't know why you won't listen to me anymore!"

"I just want to help Maison and the others," I said. "They're my friends."

"And I'm your father," he said. "You're my son. You act as if you're part of two different worlds now, but you aren't. You don't belong on Earth. You are a citizen of the Overworld. We protect our own first."

"We can protect both—" I started to say.

"You're not hearing me," Dad said. "I'm tired of you putting these—these Earth people before us. It's fine to have friends, and I'm not saying they're not good people, but you've been abandoning who you are to be with them. You've been abandoning me. I want to spend a single day with you after all we've been through lately, and all you can think about is Maison, Maison, Maison. In any case, your friends aren't trained to fight mobs, so all they'd do is get in the way."

"That's not true!" I argued. "Maison and Destiny and Yancy have all fought mobs!"

"They haven't fought a Wither," he said. "You saw what it did to our home in a matter of seconds. This is destruction beyond what your friends understand. And normal Withers can't go through portals, let alone use portals to create this." He angrily gestured to the land around us. "This is a Herobrine-made Wither, which makes it even more dangerous than any other Wither. I couldn't believe you earlier, rushing up to it with a block, thinking you could defeat it. You're lucky I got to you in time. Now stop this nonsense and come with me to the village!"

Before I could say a word, I heard a terrible cry, and several ghasts shot out of nowhere, their eyes on us.

CHAPTER 6

"**L**OOK OUT!" DAD SAID.

Ghasts were square-shaped mobs that flew through the sky and spat fireballs. I dove out of the way of the first fireball, missing it by inches. Dad slashed out with his diamond pickaxe, hitting a blast of fire and shooting it right back at the ghast. The fire hit right on target, taking the ghast out immediately.

I was trying to do the same with my sword, but it took skill and aim. More ghasts flew overhead, raining blast after blast of fire down on us. Dad was successfully hitting the fireballs back at them while all I could do was dodge and try to hit back. There were so many of them!

And then it got worse. From behind the portal house stepped a whole row of wither skeletons, all of them armed with black swords. Their angry-looking skulls reminded me of the three skull faces on the Wither.

"Get the skeletons, Stevie!" Dad called, not pausing in his battle against the ghasts. I obeyed, running toward the pack of wither skeletons. Ossie, who had been sitting on my shoulder, jumped down and ran for cover.

I swung my sword out, hitting two wither skeletons. Two more rose up over me, and I slashed at them, knocking them back but not defeating them. The wither skeletons leapt toward me again as I continued to fling my sword out. If a wither skeleton touched me, it would give me the wither effect, draining me of my strength. As it was, I could barely handle them. The wither skeletons were all over me, bearing down, barely giving me any room to swing my sword. I took one out with a quick stab and knocked another back.

"Stevie, duck!" Dad shouted.

I ducked. The fireball that had been aimed for me hit a wither skeleton instead, causing it to vanish. Ducking had saved me from the ghast's fire, but it also put me into a very awkward position. One of the wither skeleton's black swords came out and knocked my diamond sword right out of my hand. I lunged for the sword, though I already knew it would be too late. The two remaining skeletons loomed over me, swords at the ready.

CHAPTER 7

AT THE LAST MOMENT, ARROWS STRUCK BOTH wither skeletons, one after the other. For a second I lay there, trembling, watching as the arrows hit their mark and the wither skeletons turned red and disappeared.

And then I saw my cousin Alex just ahead, drawing back her bow. With graceful ease, she sent several more arrows flying, taking out the rest of the ghasts over Dad.

"Alex!" Dad said in amazement.

"Looks like I got here just in time, Uncle Steve," Alex said brightly. I could tell she was really proud of herself. Then again, she had every reason to be.

"What are you doing here?" Dad asked. What we really owed Alex right then was a thank you, but Dad was already preoccupied with other things. "Where is your mother?"

Before Alex could answer, I saw that the portal house's door was open, and that Maison, Destiny, and Yancy were running out of it.

"You guys are all right!" I exclaimed, hurrying over. "Has Earth been affected like this too?"

"No!" Maison said. "Yancy and Destiny were over at my place, and then Alex just fell out through the computer screen." Maison's computer was where we always came from when we went through the Earth portal.

"I was out exploring when the whole land turned red," Alex told Dad. "I wasn't far from where you and Stevie live, so I ran over there. When I saw your house was destroyed and you were nowhere around, I ran to get Maison to help look for you."

"We must have just missed each other," Dad said.

"I'm so glad you're okay," Maison said breathlessly. "We were so scared when Alex told us what was happening."

"Did you see the Wither?" I asked Alex. Ossie came running back to us now that the battle was done, and I picked her up.

"A Wither is causing this?" Alex said, wide-eyed.

I quickly filled them in, trying not to notice Dad's annoyed look. He wasn't going to tell Maison, Destiny, and Yancy to leave now that they were here, though it was obvious he wasn't pleased.

"That Wither we saw in the Nether did this?" Alex cried. "But Withers can't go through portals!"

"This one can," I said bitterly. "Because of Herobrine."

"Kids, we don't have time to stand here and talk," Dad cut in. "We need to get to the village."

No one argued with that, and we all started heading in the direction of the village. I noticed that Maison had brought along her baseball bat, and Yancy and Destiny had grabbed wooden swords for themselves before going through the portal.

"I wonder why the Wither didn't believe you were, well, *you*," Destiny said, mulling over this.

"I don't know," I said. "I'm more worried about its connection with Herobrine. I knew it was too good to be true that Herobrine was gone!"

"Herobrine is gone," Yancy said. "And it doesn't sound as if this Wither is too bright, even if it can talk. I actually think defeating Withers in the game is pretty fun . . ." He trailed off when he saw that Dad was glaring at him.

"Fun?" Dad repeated. "Fun? Come look at the condition our house is in. Look at the condition the Overworld is in! It's just a game for you, but this is our world. I don't think you understand that."

Yancy clammed up, uncomfortable.

"We get destruction on Earth too," Maison said. "There was actually just an earthquake near us that ruined some people's houses. Yancy, Destiny, and I were all meeting up because we were going to go over there and help rebuild."

This caught Dad's attention. "An earthquake? Is that like a Wither? Does it seek out things to destroy?"

"Well, no," Maison said.

"Do you create it using ingredients like wither skulls and soul sand?" Dad went on. No matter how many times I told Dad about Earth, he still couldn't fathom it being that different from the Overworld.

"Earthquakes are about faults and seismic waves," Yancy said. "It's science, not magic."

"We felt the earthquake where we live," Maison said. "Then we heard on the news that some people lost their houses, and adults were going to go help them rebuild. So we thought we'd join up. None of us lost anything in the earthquake."

Dad grunted. I wasn't really sure what that meant.

"Don't worry, we'll take care of the Wither first," Yancy said. "Those houses will still be there when we get back. On the other hand . . ." Then he stopped. I guess he realized it wouldn't be good for him to continue that sentence, because it was probably something along the lines of, "On the other hand, the Overworld might not be here if we don't do something now."

It was something I believe we were all thinking, and none of us wanted to say. And when we reached the village near my house, we realized just how bad things were.

CHAPTER 8

THE VILLAGE HAD BEEN LEVELED. BITS AND parts of houses remained, but whole homes had been knocked to the ground. In the midst of the carnage, people were either trying to put their homes back together, or they were fighting against Nether mobs that had snuck up on them. It was a devastating sight.

Dad spotted the blacksmith standing near the front of the village, attempting to fix a destroyed house. Dad regularly visited the blacksmith to trade emeralds for supplies, and now he rushed over to his friend.

"Steve!" the blacksmith exclaimed when he saw Dad. "It's good to know you're safe."

"Same to you," Dad said.

"There's an enormous Wither on a rampage!" The blacksmith shuddered at the memory. "I've never seen a Wither before, and this one was even worse than all the stories and legends I've heard about them! It was carrying a Nether portal with it, and all sorts of Nether mobs were falling out."

Dad nodded grimly. "That Wither completely destroyed my home."

"We're in the same boat then," the blacksmith said sadly. "Many people have lost their homes here. But I haven't even gotten to the strangest part. The Wither spoke! It was smashing our homes to pieces overhead and roaring that it wanted to find 'the boy with the portal.'"

Maison, Alex, Destiny, and Yancy all looked at me. I looked to the side, uncomfortable.

"What did you tell it?" Dad demanded. I knew he wanted to make sure no one in the village sent the Wither back toward me.

"We had no idea what it was talking about," the blacksmith said. "When it had leveled our village, the Wither said, 'If I can't find the boy, then first I'll find the redheaded girl. I know which village she lives in.' And it went off that way." He pointed in the direction of Alex's village. We could see a line of destruction going in that direction, too, like a morbid path.

Now everyone looked at Alex, whose face had gone sickly pale under her bright red hair. "No!" she burst out. "We have to stop it from hurting my village!"

"You need to go to that village, so what happened here doesn't happen there too," the blacksmith said to Dad. "Right now we need to stay in our village to protect it from further attacks. But you are legendary in the Overworld for your mob-slaying abilities."

"Alex," Dad said. "Perhaps you should stay here, if the Wither is looking for you."

"No way!" Alex said. "I'm not letting some evil Wither hurt my village! If that Wither wants me, it can come and get me! I've got arrows!"

"Arrows alone can't beat a Wither," Dad said. "When the Wither gets to half strength, you have to use a sword to finish it off. Arrows become useless. So if you and Stevie want to come along, you'll have to do what I say. We'll have to fight it together to have any chance of winning."

"Don't worry, we're with you!" Maison said.

Those were the wrong words to say. Dad frowned, then said to Maison, Destiny, and Yancy, "You three should go home. This doesn't concern you and you'll only be in danger."

"Doesn't concern us?" Destiny said in disbelief.

"Of course it concerns us," Yancy said.

"Stevie," Dad said. "I need to talk to you for a moment."

I exchanged bewildered looks with Alex, Maison, Destiny, and Yancy, then followed Dad to the side. He got us just far enough away that we were out of earshot of the others.

"You need to tell them to go back to Earth," he said.

"They're really good fighters," I said. I couldn't believe we were going over this again. "And talking about them is just wasting time. What if the Wither is already at Alex's village?"

"Alexandra will keep it at bay," Dad said. Aunt Alexandra was Dad's sister, Alex's mom, and also the mayor of her village. "These friends will just slow us down more. That one boy thinks fighting a Wither is just a game." His voice was full of disgust.

"I know Yancy can be a little . . . well . . . weird," I said. "But he's shown that he's an ally to the Overworld."

"Fine," Dad muttered, which surprised me. Even though I'd been arguing, I wasn't used to Dad changing his mind on things. I could tell he still wasn't happy about it. "But they're on their own. I'm not responsible for them if they're going to put themselves in such a dangerous situation."

Dad turned to the others and barked out, "Come on! We're leaving now!"

Alex and my friends exchanged more confused looks. I could see Maison, Destiny, and Yancy appeared a little intimidated by Dad, and I didn't blame them. I felt embarrassed by how he was acting.

As we hurried on, I watched Dad's face. He wouldn't look at me—he kept looking ahead. I knew part of the reason he looked ahead was to keep his eyes peeled for any nearby mobs, but it also felt as if he was refusing to look at me.

Why was that? Why was he so opposed to me spending time with my friends? And why did it feel like even though we were father and son, we couldn't be more different?

CHAPTER 9

NORMALLY IT DIDN'T TAKE ALL THAT LONG TO run from the village close to our home to Aunt Alexandra's village. However, normally we didn't have Nether mobs to deal with. Several times wither skeletons came onto our path, hissing and charging. Alex would immediately start shooting them down with arrows, and any ones she missed were taken care of by the rest of us.

"When I'm playing *Minecraft*, I like to make Withers underground, in bedrock," Yancy was saying. "That keeps them from flying up too high, and they can't destroy bedrock. I can literally defeat a Wither in a matter of seconds that way."

"Stop bragging, Yancy," Destiny said.

"It's not bragging if it's true," Yancy said. "And I love the Nether stars they drop when they're defeated. They make for great beacons, and I like to decorate with them."

Dad's face twitched. He was not amused by Yancy still talking about a Wither as if it were a game. Seeing Dad's angry face, Yancy quickly said, "I'm only saying this in case there's bedrock nearby. You know, maybe we can lure it there and take it out."

"There's nothing close to my village that's like that," Alex said. "I would know—I've explored every inch of the area!"

"I've never made a Wither in *Minecraft*," Destiny said. "I don't understand why you'd make something that attacks you."

"For the challenge," Yancy said brightly. "Right, Alex? You love a good challenge, don't you?"

Dad's face was twitching even harder.

"My arrows should weaken it pretty quickly, and then you can finish it off with your weapons," Alex said. Although she had seen the destruction of the village, I could tell she had already gone from being scared and pale-faced to daydreaming about what a glorious battle she'd have with the Wither. That was Alex for you—always eager for some adventure, no matter how dangerous.

She paused a moment. "Hey, Uncle Steve? How come you don't have your diamond sword?"

Instead of answering, Dad just ran faster. We had to sprint to keep up with him, and I ran over so I was right next to Alex. I tried to whisper in her ear (it's hard to whisper when you're bouncing from running), "The Wither broke his sword into pieces."

"Oh!" Alex said, looking alarmed. "Is that why he's so upset?"

I shrugged. It's also hard to shrug while bouncing from running. "I don't know what his problem is," I said. "It just feels like he's mad at me." It also felt like he really didn't like Maison, Destiny, and Yancy, but I didn't want to say that out loud and hurt their feelings.

We passed a large group of oinking zombie pigmen. Alex gave me a wicked smile. "Don't you think it's kind of funny that the Nether is back?" she said. "It's like you were in such a hurry to get out of it before, you didn't really overcome it."

I looked at my diamond sword and thought about Dad's diamond sword being smashed in the Wither's vicious mouth. "Alex," I said, because I really didn't appreciate her getting a jab at me when things were so serious. "Aren't you worried about what we're going to find when we reach your village?"

"What's all that smoke ahead?" Maison cut in, concerned.

A flurry of smoke was rising against the red sky, becoming larger and reaching across the landscape like an angry hand. We were passing many little Nether fires as we ran, but none of those could create this much smoke.

"There's a big fire ahead!" Dad said.

Alex went silent. We weren't too far from her village then. That fire couldn't be coming from her village . . . could it?

We had to rush up the blocky slopes of a mountain to see, and as we ran, the smoke grew bigger and blacker. White ghasts stood out against the dark sky, their light color shocking next to it.

When we got to the top of the mountain, what we saw was even worse than what we'd imagined. Alex's village was swept up in a furious, roaring fire, the flames swallowing up homes and spitting out ashes. Alex's house, which was on the edge of the village, was one of the homes that had been attacked. Its roof had been taken clear off, its windows shattered.

It looked as if Nether mobs had taken the place over. Wither skeletons were running from house to house, chasing out families. Ghasts shot down at people like darts of lightning and I could see the small, flaring bodies of magma cubes and blazes as they attacked people on the street.

But worst of all was the sight of the Wither. It was whirling amidst the ravaged village, its two side heads shooting skulls that blew up everything where they landed. The Wither had grown even bigger since the last time I had seen it, spreading like its own dark cloud, blocking out the sky.

"Bring me the boy with the portal!" the middle head was thundering above the roaring fire and the screams of fleeing villagers. "Bring him to me now!"

CHAPTER 10

"**Y**OU MONSTER!" ALEX HOWLED WHEN SHE SAW the scene. Now that she had witnessed this, fighting the Wither was no longer an adventure for her; it was real suffering. Just like that, she tore off down the mountain, her arrows at the ready.

"Alex, wait!" Dad called. We were all running after her. We didn't have a plan—we just knew we had to do something! Ossie jumped off my shoulder and ran for cover, which was better, because it kept her from going right into the heat of things. In the past sometimes Ossie had helped me fight mobs, and I could tell she knew she was no match for what was going on here.

"Bring me the boy with the portal!" the Wither boomed again as its two other heads continued to blast out the village with flying skulls.

Some people had run to their roofs with bows and arrows and were frantically shooting at the Wither. Either the Wither kept dodging, or ghasts flew in the way, taking the arrows instead. Then a swarm of more ghasts swept in over the people on the roofs, hitting at them with fireballs. It was a perfect distraction. If people were too busy saving themselves from the immediate attacks of wither skeletons and ghasts, they didn't have the ability to fight the Wither!

What should I do? What can I do? I thought. Maybe if I revealed myself, the Wither would stop its attack. But—but what did the Wither want with me, anyway? It wanted the portal to Earth, right? What if I showed up, and it captured me and tried to force me to tell it where the portal was?

I'll stay quiet! I promised myself. *No matter what the Wither does to me, I can't let it hurt Earth too!*

But how could I stop it from hurting the Overworld?

Then we noticed an armored woman running toward the Wither, holding a diamond sword and leading on a group of armed guards. It was Aunt Alexandra!

"Soldiers, follow me!" Aunt Alexandra called.

Her soldiers tried to hit the Wither with an explosion of arrows. It didn't work because a whole group of ghasts flew right into the line of fire. Some of the ghasts were hit by the arrows and disappeared, while others remained. Either way, none of the soldiers' arrows managed to reach the Wither. Not a single one. And now the remaining ghasts were bombarding the soldiers with fireballs, pushing them back.

Aunt Alexandra ducked out of the way and ran forward on her own to confront the Wither. One of the

Wither heads spat out another skull, and the skull hit the ground in front of her and blew up. Aunt Alexandra was knocked back, still clutching her sword. Some of the soldiers were running away from the ghasts, trying to keep from catching on fire. Her attack had been pointless, because now she had even fewer soldiers behind her, and she hadn't gotten close to the monster.

"Mom!" Alex shouted, running to Aunt Alexandra. Aunt Alexandra was coughing and pulling herself back up. As a mayor, my aunt was famous for keeping her village safe, so her struggle just showed how serious this whole situation was.

"Alex!" Aunt Alexandra exclaimed when she saw her daughter. "You're safe!"

"No one is safe right now!" Alex called back over the cries of ghasts and roars of fires. She had her bow and arrows out and started firing right away. It was no use. Ghasts burst out and took the arrows that were meant for the Wither. And I was pretty sure my eyes weren't fooling me—the Wither was actually getting bigger by the second!

"I want the boy with the portal!" the Wither wailed again, throwing out skull after skull from its two side heads. The land around it was becoming pockmarked from all the explosions. And because of the fires, the sky had gone even redder. As I ran into the scene of the attack, my ears were full of terrible sounds and my sight hazed into the color of fire. I felt my heart pounding, because I still didn't know what to do. Even if I had ideas, if I tried to shout them to Dad and the others, the Wither might hear and respond.

I realized that Herobrine was clever in his own sick, twisted way, because he'd picked the perfect mob to leave as his backup. According to what Dad had taught me, Withers craved random violence and destruction. Herobrine had given this Wither enough power and intelligence to be using some logic to achieve its ends.

As I ran toward the Wither, I told myself I had to be prepared for anything. I had to be ready to jump if it shot a skull my way. I had to be able to dodge if ghasts flew in front of me with their fireball breath. I had to be ready to run into wither skeletons, magma cubes, and all sorts of nasties from the Nether.

But I wasn't ready for what happened.

As I approached the Wither, I saw its eyes land on me. All six of them.

And suddenly it stopped spinning. It stopped throwing skulls. It just hovered there, watching me, and then three morbid grins spread across its three enormous faces.

"He's finally here," the main head said with a hiss, smiling like a snake. "The boy with the portal."

CHAPTER 11

THAT GOT ME TO FREEZE. THE BOY WITH THE PORTAL? "There is no portal!" I found myself saying as quickly as possible.

"How stupid do you think we are?" the left head demanded.

"No, no," I said. I was sweating. Was I really standing here, talking with a Wither? "You came by my house earlier. You know I'm not who you're looking for . . ."

The Wither was smiling a greasy smile as I spoke. Herobrine had always grinned in a hideous, evil way. This Wither smiled as if it thought I was being cute. And as if it might want to eat me. It wasn't a good smile.

"Oh, no. You're the boy with the portal," the middle head said.

Dad, Maison, Destiny, and Yancy had rushed up beside me. Aunt Alexandra and Alex were nearby, and everyone looked equally stunned. No one knew what was going on.

"Herobrine is just trying to trick you," I said, knowing it was a weak attempt. "That's what he does." Would the Wither believe me?

"No, you're the one trying to trick *us,*" the left head said.

"Herobrine took armies to Earth to try to take it over," the right head said. "We'll just keep the Overworld like the Nether, attack what we find, and get the portal to Earth. Do you know what we'll do then?"

I had a pretty good idea, but the middle head still told me, "We'll unleash the Nether mobs on Earth."

"There is no portal," I said. "Herobrine just fed you stories."

The Wither shook all three of its heads. "Poor, innocent little Stevie," the middle head sighed.

That sent a chill down me. *The Wither even knows my name? How much does it know?*

"Herobrine didn't tell you where this portal was, did he?" I suddenly asked. "I mean, not that it's real."

Their skull faces smiled again. "No, he didn't," the middle head replied. "But someone else did."

The Wither turned to Alex's house and all three heads began shooting skulls at it, hammering down the remaining walls. Alex cried out and tried to run toward it, only to be grabbed and held back by Aunt Alexandra. The house fell down to the base, being peeled back like a curtain, revealing layer after layer. A flurry of ghasts rushed in, and the soldiers fought back against them.

When the front wall of the house was mostly shot away, I could see inside the building.

"No," I gasped.

Standing right there was a portal to Earth.

CHAPTER 12

"**Y**OU HAVE A PORTAL?" I SAID TO ALEX, SHOCKED. As far as I knew, the portal by my house was the only portal to Earth there was! But this one looked exactly the same.

"No, I don't!" Alex shouted back. "What's that doing there?"

My head spun. If Alex hadn't known about the portal, did that mean the Wither had created an entirely new portal to Earth and just placed it in Alex's house? Why would it do that?

Then I had a terrible thought.

I sucked in a deep breath.

"Thank you for leading us right to the portal, Stevie," the middle head said with pride.

No. Oh, please, no.

"All we had to do was shoot through your house so you'd be aware of us," the middle head said. "We pretended to be ignorant about who you were, and then we flew away. Not very far away. Then we followed you all the way to the portal."

No, no, no, no. This couldn't be happening!

I looked to Dad, devastated. His face was hard and grim, but he wasn't looking at me. He was looking at the Wither.

"Now, watch this," the middle head said gleefully. "We brought the portal all this way so you could see." The Wither was still holding the Nether portal in its clutches, and zombie pigmen and wither skeletons were jumping out of it. Floating over through the sky, the Wither dropped the Nether portal into Alex's house, right next to the Earth portal.

As I watched, some wither skeletons lurched out of the Nether portal. Their dark skeleton bodies were tinged reddish in the light. They looked around for a second, as if seeking out their prey. The world they saw around them was already full of fighting. They looked at the Earth portal, shimmering red, green, and blue in front of them, full of promise.

The wither skeletons didn't even need instructions. Holding their black swords high, they walked right through my portal to Earth. More wither skeletons came out of the Nether portal then, and they followed the wither skeletons in front of them. Once they got through the Earth portal, they'd land in Maison's bedroom. They'd walk through her house and out the door. And then they'd find a whole new world there, ready for the taking.

CHAPTER 13

COULDN'T LET THIS HAPPEN! I BEGAN TO CHARGE forward. The Wither burst out laughing, enjoying my panic.

"What do you think, Stevie?" the middle head called out.

Then it began shooting skulls again. A skull came bursting toward me and I dove to the side, barely escaping the impact. More screams and shouts arose as people tried to battle back the mobs. A few people had grabbed their most important belongings and were running from the village, as if they didn't think they had a chance otherwise.

I got back up to my feet and a wither skeleton jumped in front of me. Wither skeletons are much taller than regular skeletons in the Overworld, and I shuddered to think about Earth being overrun by them. This wither skeleton brought its sword down and I threw my sword up, the two blades screeching against each other.

I pushed with all my might, and when the wither skeleton fell back, I hit it with my sword. It vanished.

Before I could really get my bearings, several ghasts appeared overhead, opening their mouths and sending their fire straight at me. I dove again, then turned back with my sword. With a swing, I hit a fire blast on my first try. The fire flew back at the ghast who'd spat it, hitting perfectly. However, that still left three more ghasts above me, and I was jumping around, trying not to get hit. If only I could take care of these stupid ghasts and reach the Wither!

As I dodged and hit at fire blasts, I tried to think of what I needed to do next. *Think, Stevie, think!* Too many Nether mobs were keeping people from going after the Wither. More Nether mobs were heading to Earth right at this very moment.

My first thought was to destroy the portal to Earth, because then the people there would only have to take care of the handful of wither skeletons that had slipped through. That was still better than this onslaught that kept coming out of the Nether portal and going through the Earth portal.

But there was one really major, important reason why I couldn't just go up and destroy that portal. The portal was one of a kind. I'd been able to remake it once before, but only after a dangerous trip through the Nether. I didn't even know what the Nether looked like now, since the Overworld looked like this. Would the Nether be the same? Would I be able to find the same stones to make a new Earth portal? I couldn't let myself destroy that portal—that would trap Maison, Yancy, and Destiny in my world!

Then that left the Nether portal. It obviously needed to be destroyed, because that would stop all these mobs from getting out. And it also seemed to me like the Wither was seriously attached to it, and the Wither *had* mentioned using Herobrine's powers to make the portal special and allow all this to happen. Did that mean that destroying the portal might destroy the Wither, or at least weaken it so we could finish it off?

An arrow struck one of the ghasts above me, and I caught sight of Alex out of the corner of my eye. I still didn't know where everyone else had gone. A few more shots, and Alex had cleared out all the ghasts by me. This also cleared me a narrow path.

"Thank you, Alex!" I shouted. I had to get to that Nether portal! Sword held close, I went running toward Alex's house.

I was just about there when a skull flew in front of my face. The next thing I knew, the ground between me and the house was gone, smashed out. I was knocked back, but I wasn't giving up. Most of the walls had been stripped away, with a few blocks remaining like little jagged ledges. Grabbing the ledge, I hoisted myself up and tumbled into the remains of Alex's living room. Now the two portals were within a few feet of me.

Zombie pigmen were ambling through the room, and I tried to push through them as quickly as I could without hurting them in any way. The zombie pigmen oinked as I jostled them, but otherwise left me alone.

A wither skeleton was just emerging from the Nether portal as I approached. Seeing me, it advanced like a soldier, its sword at the ready. I swung at it with my sword, the two of us wrestling, then I knocked it back and hit it. Before any more Nether mobs could get through, I stepped up close to the Nether portal and raised my sword.

And before I could bring my sword down and destroy the portal, I felt someone—or something—grab me and lift me straight into the air.

CHAPTER 14

I'D BEEN CAUGHT IN THE MOUTH OF THE WITHER!
Out of nowhere the enormous left head of the
Wither had dived down into Alex's living room,
snatching me up by the back of my shirt. In seconds I
was high above the roofless house.

Down below I saw Maison hoist herself over the
blocks and get into the living room. She jumped
through the Earth portal, her bat raised. She must have
run there to take out the mobs in her house and keep
any more from getting in. Her timing was just right
for that. But it had also been the worst timing, since
she'd arrived *right* after I'd been grabbed. She hadn't
seen what had happened to me, so she couldn't help!

Slowly, the left head moved so that it was facing the
other two Wither heads. The right head was still shooting skulls in every direction, but the middle head had
its sharp white eyes on me. At this point the Wither
had gotten so big that the lines of its eyes were bigger

than my sword. Grasped in its clutches, I shuddered at the sheer size of this monster.

I tried to slash the middle head with my blade. My hands were fumbling so badly I did about the worst thing I could have done—I dropped my diamond sword. I couldn't see where it fell, but as soon as I felt that sword drop from my hand, I knew I was doomed.

"Did you really think we were going to let you ruin our portal?" the middle head mocked me.

Where were Alex and her arrows? Where was Dad? Where were Yancy and Destiny—or anyone else? I tried to look around and I saw villagers running, ghasts flying, fires raging, and more skulls being thrown from the Wither's right head. I saw a red sky and a Nether-like land as far as my eyes could see. I didn't see anyone I knew. I didn't see any good way out of this.

What I did see was the ground below. Far, far below. Maybe if I could get the Wither to drop me, I'd be able to grab its body and slide down it. It would break my fall, but could I actually make that work?

My hand went into my tool kit, trying to find a weapon, trying to remember what I'd shoved in there earlier. My hand closed around a sword handle. Yes! This had to work! I ripped the sword out of my tool kit, wanting to scare the Wither with it.

When I saw what I had grabbed, I had the most awful feeling. It was the handle of my broken wooden sword. It was useless!

The middle head burst out laughing again. "You poor fool!" it shouted. "*This* is the boy who defeated Herobrine? This is a child with a child's toy! A child's *broken* toy!"

The right head stopped shooting skulls long enough to look over and get in a good laugh too. Even the head holding me was starting to shake because it was cracking up. The left head couldn't take it anymore, and its mouth opened so it could laugh uproariously. Just like that, I was released, plummeting to the ground with my useless sword. The Wither was laughing too hard to even bother to watch me drop. Why did it need to keep track of me, anyway? It knew this battle was over.

CHAPTER 15

BUT INSTEAD OF HITTING THE HARD GROUND, I found myself landing on something soft. Soft? I looked around me dizzily and realized I'd landed on a bed piled high with blankets. What were the odds of that?

Then I saw Dad at the edge of the bed, and realized he'd pushed it right under me so I'd fall on it. I'd lost track of the others, but he hadn't lost track of me.

"Dad," I rasped, shocked. He was picking up my diamond sword from where it had fallen.

"Let's go, Stevie," he said, and grabbed me. I tried to protest. Ignoring this, Dad rushed us out of the craziness and out of the village, my legs unsteady and tripping after my experience in the Wither's mouth. Each time I almost fell, Dad gripped me harder and kept me on my feet.

"Look, the boy with the portal is running away!" the middle head laughed.

"I told you he didn't stand a chance against us!" the left head roared.

"Bye-bye, portal boy!" the right head hollered.

All three heads began to chant at me in unison, "You're a fool! You're a fool!"

"Dad, what are we doing?" I cried in a whisper. I was trying to ignore the Wither's taunts as we fled, but its words wouldn't stop chanting in my mind, even after the Wither stopped talking. "We can't abandon everyone!"

"Trust me, Stevie," Dad said. "We're in over our heads there."

I couldn't believe I was hearing this. "We're just leaving everyone to fend for themselves?"

Dad gave me a sharp look and didn't answer. I couldn't understand this. All my life I'd grown up with stories about my Dad being a feared mob slayer. Were they not true? What kind of feared mob slayer ran away?

We came to a half-broken, empty house near the village and Dad hustled me inside. The walls only gave cold comfort, because while it was better than no safety, the Wither still could burn down these walls and get to us if it wanted to.

"Dad, we can't leave!" I said. "I almost had that Wither! We can still get it!"

The look Dad gave me was even worse now. "*Almost had the Wither!*" he exclaimed. "That Wither almost had *you!*"

I put my head down. "I had other weapons in my tool kit. If I'd had a few more seconds to reach for one—"

"With Withers, you don't have a few more seconds," Dad said. "I fought a Wither once as a young man, and it almost killed me."

I stopped and stared. Since I was little, it felt as if Dad had told me a million stories about his adventures fighting mobs. But I didn't know *this* story.

"Someone thought it would be a good joke to make a Wither," Dad said with contempt. "Of course the Wither got out of control and started attacking people and ruining houses."

"What did you do?" I asked.

"Actually, what your friend Yancy suggested," Dad said. "I got it to chase me into an area with bedrock. I was badly hurt, but it worked. Unfortunately, the closest bedrock from here . . ." He trailed off and shook its head. It was too far away to have a Wither chase us there.

"We can't just leave the village like this," I said.

Dad looked taken aback by my words. "We're not leaving the village," he said. "I just got us out to a safer area so we can plan. With a Wither like this, it's going to take more than strength. We need a strategy."

I felt some hope now. I knew Dad wouldn't abandon everyone! "But what are we going to do?" I asked.

"I sent your friend Maison through the Earth portal," Dad said, "to take care of the mobs that got through. I told Yancy and Destiny to join her. That should keep *that* situation under control for a little bit."

So that's why I saw Maison run there! "Where are Alex and Aunt Alexandra?"

"They're trying to get the soldiers back together," Dad said. "However, the soldiers are panicking and not listening to Alexandra's instructions. If they'd stop, think through things, and listen to her, they'd be doing better."

I had a feeling Dad was also kind of implying that I needed to think through things and listen to *him* better. I thought about being grabbed by the Wither and I blushed again.

"I was just trying to destroy the Nether portal!" I said. "I figured maybe it would weaken the Wither! The Wither takes that portal with it everywhere, so there must be some connection."

"It was good thinking, but the way you tried to destroy it was reckless," Dad said. "Just like when you attacked the Wither at our house."

Outside, the screams and hisses got even louder, as if something especially bad had just happened. I shuddered.

"We need to take out both the Wither and the portal," Dad said. "As long as they're close together, the Wither will keep protecting the portal. It will have no reason to move."

He glanced out the window. "Look out, Stevie!" Before I could respond, he pushed me out of the way. A skull crashed through the wall and landed right by us. We really weren't safe anywhere.

Think, Stevie! I was screaming in my mind. *You've stopped a zombie takeover! You got Yancy out of a dungeon when he was arrested. You even stopped Herobrine!*

I thought about the Wither mocking me. *"Look, the boy with the portal is running away!"* The memory of its laughter clouded my thoughts and made me angry. I needed to prove that darn Wither wrong, to show it I could fight mobs and do the right thing!

Wait a second.

My brain started to turn into a new direction. Something clicked into place. I felt a rush as an idea swept over me.

"Dad?" I said a little hesitantly.

"What?"

I whispered the words so there was no chance of the Wither overhearing, because I didn't know how good its hearing was. "I think I might know how to defeat the Wither."

CHAPTER 16

I TOOK A DEEP BREATH. "WE NEED TO HAVE A TWO-pronged attack. We're going to split off into different groups, but if we don't all do our share, it won't work."

I had Dad's full attention, and he nodded as if he approved of this. "What do we do?"

"Maison, Yancy, and Destiny are already taking care of the Earth portal by stopping mobs there," I said. "We need to get the Wither away from the Nether portal. Then Aunt Alexandra and Alex can sneak over without the Wither standing guard and destroy the Nether portal."

"That's good," Dad said. "But how do you get the Wither away?"

I took another deep breath. "You know the dungeon Aunt Alexandra has in this village for criminals? Well, one time Yancy got arrested and thrown into that dungeon, and we all broke him out."

Dad was frowning now. "What does this have to do with anything?"

"The dungeon is underground," I said. "It won't work as well as bedrock, but it's still an enclosed space. The Wither can't fly up and away if we get it in there. I mean, the Wither is so big now that if it gets into the dungeon, it'll barely be able to move, let alone fly."

Now I saw Dad's eyes light up. "I like it," he said. "The Wither could still fly backward and get out, but if we keep it distracted, it won't get a chance. Still, how do we get it in there?"

"Well, I guess that's the hardest part," I said. "We have to get the Wither to chase us there, and then we can finish it off."

Now Dad was looking skeptical. "How do we get it to chase us? It got your portal. It even got to show you what it's doing with it. We're no longer special to the Wither."

"Wait, I know!" I said, thinking of the bed Dad had used to break my fall. If Dad could make something work in a way it's not supposed to, then we could do that again. "When we were last in the dungeon, there was all sorts of junk on the floor. What if we take those scraps and . . . and . . . turn them into a portal?"

Dad looked at me as if I was babbling in another language.

"Not a real portal!" I said. "Just something that looks like a portal. What if the Wither thinks I have *another* portal, one that leads to *another* new world?

Why would it stop at just attacking Earth if it thinks it can get to other worlds too?"

"Hmm, I think you have something there," Dad said. "But how do we convince the Wither that there's another portal?"

We didn't have time to figure that out. Because just then a tall monster broke into the house, holding a raised sword.

CHAPTER 17

I BELLOWED IN SURPRISE, THEN SAW IT WAS ONLY Yancy. I was so jumpy I'd expected the worst!

"Stevie, you're all right!" Yancy said, sounding relieved.

"What's going on?" I asked.

"Maison and Destiny went through the portal and are fighting mobs coming through to Maison's house," he said. "I haven't seen Alexandra, and no one can get close to attacking the Wither because it keeps a steady supply of Nether mobs in the way. It just laughs and shoots skulls. Alex is still trying to battle through those mobs to get to the Wither and isn't having any luck. I was hurrying to the Earth portal to help Maison and Destiny out, but then I saw Stevie fall and get carried off, so I followed. I would have been here sooner if so many Nether mobs hadn't gotten in my way!"

I filled him in on our idea, down to the portal-building part.

"I'm in!" Yancy said. "Tell me how I can help!"

"We need to figure out how to convince the Wither there's another portal," Dad said. "If we just walk up there and tell it that, it wouldn't have any reason to believe us."

Yancy thought about it for a moment. "I've got it!" he said. "I'll convince it."

"You?" Dad didn't try to hide his skepticism.

"You two run to the dungeon and start making that portal," Yancy said. "It shouldn't take long. While you're doing that, I'll go tell the Wither I'm from another world, one that's not Earth. I'll convince it that I want to be on its side and you're hiding the portal in the dungeon. By the time the Wither arrives, the 'portal' will already be made. The Wither explodes through some bars to let itself in, and—BAM!— you've got yourself a Wither in a tight space!"

"Except you look like someone from Earth," I said. "And the Wither saw you come running up with me. It'll know you're not my enemy."

Yancy shook one of his long fingers at me as if I were being silly. He was smiling. "I got two things to help me out. First, sound effects." He pulled his cell phone out of his pocket. "The Wither won't know that my cell phone is really making noise. It'll think I'm making all sorts of crazy noises because, well, I'm from a different world."

"Okay, okay, good," I said.

"Two." Yancy held up two fingers. "I have the perfect disguise."

He gestured toward the doorway. Just outside the house was a garden full of Jack o' Lanterns.

"You're going to hide who you are by putting a Jack o' Lantern on your head!" I said, realizing. Yancy had disguised himself in the Overworld that way before too. The only problem was that it was very hard for him to see out the eyeholes in the pumpkin. At this point, though, we were all willing to take that risk.

The next thing I knew, Alex had stormed into the house. "Yancy!" she shouted. "You don't get to run away! We need all the help we can get!"

My heart leapt excitedly. Now we didn't have to go looking for Alex! I told her our plan, and she immediately said, "Count me in. Here." She shoved keys into my hands. When I gave her a baffled look, she said, "One of those keys is to the dungeon! My mom gave me the village keys to get more weapons from warehouses, but your idea sounds better. I'm going to run and find my mom. She has a diamond pickaxe that will make short work of that Nether portal!"

I nodded eagerly, hoping we could make this work. Yancy was setting the Jack o' Lantern on his head and it made him look ridiculous. "Do I look like I'm from another world?" he asked, striking a pose with his hands on his hips.

"Model later," Alex said, shoving him out the door while Dad and I quickly followed. "Let's do this!"

CHAPTER 18

DAD HANDED MY DIAMOND SWORD BACK TO ME, and then we went skidding through the rust-tinted landscape, dodging magma cubes and jumping away from ghast fireballs. We didn't have time to stop and fight. We needed to get to that dungeon!

The Wither saw us running and howled with laughter. "Look, the boy with the portal is fleeing again!" the middle head said.

"He must be looking for another pathetic wooden sword," the left head said.

"Run, boy, run!" the right head said.

The dungeon was on the edge of the village, not too far from us. A few blocks had been knocked from its top edges, like bites taken out of the stone; other than that, though, it was in one piece, which was pretty amazing. Most of the building was underground, with more blocks on top of it, preventing people from escaping.

We ducked behind the building, out of the Wither's sight. Balancing my diamond sword in one hand, I desperately went through the keys Alex had given me. There were so many, and she hadn't told me which one opened the dungeon! I started trying key after key, in order. None of them were working.

While I did this, Dad kept us safe. Some wither skeletons skulked up, and when I started to turn, Dad said, "Never mind them! Find the right key!"

He ran toward the wither skeletons with his diamond pickaxe and defeated them in a matter of seconds. Despite the fact I only caught it out of the corner of my eye, I was impressed. Even though I'd had some moments questioning what Dad did, his fight with the wither skeletons reminded me what a good mob slayer he was.

Finally, I inserted a key that worked. The door to the dungeon opened and Dad and I rushed inside, closing the door behind us.

Inside the dungeon it was dank and scary. The red light from outside made the bars create strange, creepy shadows on the ground. Just like before, the dungeon was littered with all kinds of random materials people had discarded here.

"Get to work!" Dad said.

I picked up some blocks. How were we going to make this happen? None of the blocks matched.

"Just stack the blocks," Dad said, seeing my hesitance. So I did. I created the outline of a portal, while

Dad got us some bars from the windows. He put the bars along the edge of the "portal," making it look especially vicious, even if the blocks didn't fit together.

"What do we do for the middle?" I asked. Normally, if I were making a portal I'd use flint and steel in the middle. My eyes fell on the few torches that lined the dungeon walls, and that got me thinking. Snatching up the torches, I outlined the center of the "portal." This didn't spark up a real portal, but it made an eerie glow. It also made the rest of the dungeon even darker, so that the glowing in our make-believe "portal" seemed all the more bright and believable.

We stepped back and looked at our work.

Dad seemed to know what I was thinking. "It doesn't have to look good as long as it works as a trick," he said. "What's going on outside?"

We pushed some blocks over to a still-barred window so we could stand on them and look outside. In the far corner of our vision, I could see Alex rushing over to Aunt Alexandra, who was still trying to get her soldiers in order. Alex was jumping up and down, and when Aunt Alexandra heard her words, I saw her eyes widen.

And then there was Yancy, walking right up to the Wither.

I think Yancy was trying to strut in that cool, confident way of his. Unfortunately, the Jack o' Lantern mask wasn't really helping that effect. It was messing up his eyesight so much that he was moving in a tipsy, funny manner. He also had his cell phone making all sorts of noises, acting as if it were coming from him. I heard a duck quack, an alarm clock go off, and a police siren start blaring. Oh, Yancy.

As he drew closer, all three pairs of the Wither's eyes landed on him.

"Who—or *what*—are you?" demanded the middle head. "Your body and way of speaking are strange to us."

Yancy stopped walking and examined his fingers. I bet he couldn't actually see his fingers, but he was using a gesture I'd seen people use in Earth movies. He was acting like he was so bored that he was checking out his nails.

"Oh, I'm just from a different world," Yancy sighed, his voice a little muffled by the Jack o' Lantern. "I wondered why you didn't chase after the boy with the portal."

"We have no more use for that boy," the middle head replied. "We have his portal."

"You have *a* portal," Yancy said. "But that Stevie guy, he doesn't just have portals to one world."

"You mean he has a portal to the End?" the left head asked.

"No, no, I mean he has a portal to Yancytopia," Yancy said.

Even though it was a heart-pounding moment, I wanted to roll my eyes. Leave it to Yancy!

"Yancytopia?" the three heads asked one another, dumbfounded.

"It's a new world, one even Herobrine didn't know about," Yancy said. "I'm from there. They call me King Yancy."

Dad turned and looked at me in frustrated disbelief. "*This* is who we're counting on?" he asked. "He still thinks this is a game!"

"Why are you telling us this?" the right head hissed.

Yancy examined his nails some more. "Oh, because I'm awfully tired of Yancytopia the way it is. I think it'd be a lot more fun if it had Nether mobs running through it. Or maybe you could come visit too."

"You want us to destroy your world?" the middle head asked in surprise. It started to look skeptical.

"Or, you know, you can just do this whole red thing, with lava and fires and wither skeletons," Yancy said. "I think it's some nice interior decorating."

The Wither heads all looked at one another again.

"Can you believe this?" asked the left head.

"His world probably would look better with lava and fires," said the right head. "Look how ugly he is. I can't imagine how ugly his world would be."

"Stevie didn't really run away," Yancy went on, ignoring all that. "He just went to try to hide his other portal from you. I'd like to show you where it is. I figure maybe the two of us could work together. Or would it be the four of us? Does each one of your heads count as its own person? Never mind."

"We are interested in this portal," the middle head said. "Take us to it."

It began to rise up from where it had been hovering, leaving the Nether portal and Earth portals behind. Yancy was being his usual weird self, and the Wither was falling for it!

"It's right this way," Yancy said, starting to jog toward the dungeon.

As Dad and I watched, barely breathing, Yancy and the Wither drew closer. Once the Wither had gotten out of the immediate area it'd been staying in, I saw Aunt Alexandra and Alex rush for the Nether portal, battling against ghasts as they went. Would they make it to the portal? Would they get rid of it in time?

We had no idea, because suddenly the whole scene was blocked from us by the approaching Wither. Yancy reached the dungeon and pointed to it. "Stevie and his dad are hiding right in there," he said.

The Wither lowered its three heads. Dad and I ducked down from the window and pressed ourselves against the dank dungeon wall so that it wouldn't see us.

"There is a portal in there!" exclaimed the left head. "It's the strangest looking portal I've ever seen."

"He's not lying, but I don't trust him," said the right head. "Why would he lead us to his portal?"

"Thank you, King Yancy of Yancytopia," the middle head said in a lordly voice. "We will enjoy using this portal to your world."

"No problem," Yancy said.

It was working so well! Slowly I peeked just the top of my head over the window. The Wither had straightened its body and was looking at Jack o' Lantern Yancy.

When I saw the smiles start to spread over all three of the Wither's faces, I knew that something bad was about to happen.

"There's one more thing, King Yancy," the middle head declared. "We have to give you a reward for showing this to us."

"Yancy, look out!" I shouted as I saw the three Wither mouths opening to shoot a barrage of skulls. Yancy tried to run, only to stumble and trip because he couldn't see well. He fell on his hands and knees—helpless before the Wither. And then it seemed as if the world exploded.

CHAPTER 19

"**Y**ANCY!" I SHOUTED AGAIN. DAD GRABBED ME and threw us both to the ground. Two of the skulls the Wither had hurled hit the dungeon, knocking blocks away to make room for the Wither's entrance.

"Stay down!" Dad ordered when I attempted to scramble back up.

"No!" I said. "No! They hit Yancy!"

The next thing I knew, more blocks had been blown out of the dungeon wall, and the Wither's three heads were pushing into the underground room with us. Almost at once they saw where Dad and I were crouched down.

"This portal is ours!" shouted the middle head, hissing at us.

A new rain of skulls came bursting out of the Wither's mouths, destroying blocks behind us and around us. But the dungeon as a whole was staying in place, and the low ceiling prevented the Wither from being able to move much.

I realized there was no chance I could get to Yancy with the Wither in the way. Our only hope was to defeat the Wither and then rush to my wounded friend's aid. *Hold on, Yancy!* I thought, as if he could hear me. *We're coming for you!* Dad and I were dodging the Wither's skulls, trying to get close enough to the Wither to attack it with our weapons.

Another blast! I leapt away from a skull and it hit the wall behind me, exploding. The Wither was pushing itself deeper in at the same time that it was trying to hit us. Dad managed to reach one of the heads and he drew back his diamond pickaxe and struck hard.

"There's no use fighting us!" the middle head roared. "You're all doomed, and that new portal is ours!"

I rolled to dodge a skull and found I'd rolled right up to the left head. Before that head could respond, I was slashing at it with my sword. The Wither hissed and jerked away, letting loose another skull. However, with the Wither so closed in now, it was having a harder time moving its heads where it wanted. That meant it had a harder time aiming the skulls.

Then the Wither emitted a hideous screech of anger and shock. It was so loud Dad and I both automatically jumped back, as if we expected the screech to hurt us. The three Wither heads tried to look behind it, to see what was going on outside.

And I couldn't believe it. Through the holes in the walls, I saw a blue sky! The Nether mobs had all vanished! In the distance were Aunt Alexandra and Alex, their weapons still at the ready, standing next to where the Nether portal had been. They'd destroyed it!

"No!" the Wither heads shrieked all at once. "My portal! How did you know that's what held the power to create a Nether in the Overworld?"

Then the three heads turned and looked at Dad and me with renewed fury.

"You might have taken my Nether portal, but I still have the Earth portal!" the middle head shouted. "And I'll get that portal to the new world!"

"Just you try!" Dad shouted back.

The Wither screeched and dove forward, but I could see that its body was shrinking, as if its power was running out. I'd been right that the Nether portal, the Nether landscape, and the Wither were all connected!

"Stevie, now!" Dad yelled.

I rushed at the Wither, slashing at it with my sword so fast the blue blade seemed as if it were flying.

Outside, the villagers were realizing there were no more Nether mobs to fear. Maison jumped out of the Earth portal, followed by Destiny, looking around. They must have noticed no more mobs were coming through the Earth portal, and come back to the Overworld to investigate.

Almost at once the villagers, Aunt Alexandra, Alex, Maison, and Destiny caught sight of where the real battle was. And almost at once they all raised their weapons and came running toward the Wither.

The Wither heard the shouts of the villagers as they were dashing toward us. This made it all the more angry. When the left head saw its skulls weren't reaching me, it tried to seize me in its mouth. I jumped out of the way, accidentally dropping my toolkit in the process.

"You haven't won yet!" the middle head thundered at Dad. "I took your diamond sword! I took your house! I will take your son next!"

All three heads veered toward me, open-mouthed. I vaulted to the side, knocking myself against the wall, but missing their bites. Villagers were crowded around the dungeon from the outside, shooting arrows. I heard someone shout, "The arrows aren't working anymore!"

"That means it's at half strength!" Dad exclaimed. "We've almost got it! Only weapons like swords can finish a Wither off at this point!"

The villagers put down their arrows and rushed in with swords.

"You can take my diamond sword and you can take my house, but you'll never have my son!" Dad hollered as he dove at the Wither with his pickaxe. Raising my sword, I followed. Everyone was attacking the trapped Wither at once. Dad and I both charged with our weapons, striking the hissing Wither. The Wither let out one final cry of vengeance, but it was too late. It vanished into the air, dropping a Nether star on the dungeon floor.

CHAPTER 20

THE VILLAGERS BEGAN CHEERING, JUMPING UP and down. But my eyes instantly sought out Yancy, and I saw him still lying right where he'd fallen. In the explosions, he'd lost his Jack o' Lantern mask, and his pale skin had gone so white it looked like the clouds drifting overhead. He wasn't moving at all.

No! We're too late!

I pushed through the villagers, needing to reach him. People were in my way, too excited about their victory to see the wounded person on the ground.

Alex, Maison, and Destiny were all standing together cheering on the other side of the dungeon because they didn't even know what had happened to Yancy. When they saw my frantic face, their eyes must have followed where I was going, because then I heard Alex cry, "Oh no, Yancy!"

I pushed through more people and then I was standing over Yancy's body. I was stunned at what I was seeing. "Dad!" I said.

Dad had been the first to reach Yancy's side, and he was slowly lifting him up. Yancy's head fell back, his hair especially dark against the whiteness of his face. His eyes were peacefully closed and his mouth was slightly open.

Then I realized Dad had grabbed my tool kit from where it had fallen in the dungeon. As I watched, he pulled the Potion of Healing out of it. Gently, as if he were nursing a wounded soldier back to health, he poured the contents into Yancy's mouth. I couldn't believe the look on my dad's face as he tried to heal Yancy—he was like a totally different person from the one who had scowled at Yancy earlier.

"What happened?" Destiny cried, falling on her knees next to Yancy and Dad. "Is he going to be okay?" Yancy was her cousin, and I could see she was struggling not to cry. Alex and Maison stood overhead, horrified and speechless.

"He led the Wither over to the dungeon so we could trap it," Dad said. "And the Wither hit him before he could get away."

"Yancy!" Alex got down and yelled in his ear. "This isn't funny! Wake up!"

"He did a very brave thing for us," Dad said quietly. "I was wrong when I accused him of thinking this was all a game."

The battle wasn't supposed to end like this! We'd beaten the Wither, but I couldn't celebrate with Yancy in this sort of shape. I remembered how I used to hate Yancy, how we'd been enemies. Then we'd become wary allies, then finally friends. And after all that, I was just going to lose him?

That's when Yancy started to cough. As we all watched in wonder, he sat up hacking and sputtering, the color rushing back to his face.

"Oh, Yancy!" Destiny said, still looking as if she could cry, but now from relief and joy. I saw Maison breathe a sigh of relief and Alex just about jumped on Yancy, shaking him by the shirt and exclaiming, "Don't you scare us like that! You're always scaring us! It's not funny, you know!"

"Wow," Yancy said. His voice was kind of frail. "I didn't know I'd gotten so popular."

I smiled. Clearly Yancy was going to be okay, with the help of rest and food.

Alex huffed. She would never outright say she was glad Yancy was safe, but judging from Yancy's small smile, he knew we were all glad for him.

"This is nice," Yancy said softly. "Having people who really care about you, I mean. I feel like I went for years without having friends. And now . . ." His eyes trailed over us and he just smiled more. "Thank you, guys."

"And that," Dad said to me, "is why you always bring along a Potion of Healing."

CHAPTER 21

AFTER WE'D DEFEATED THE WITHER, AUNT ALEXANdra, Alex, and their fellow villagers began rebuilding their homes. Ossie came out of hiding, safe and sound. Without all the Nether mobs attacking them, it didn't take long for the villagers to fix up their places well enough for the night. They would take care of the extra work in the morning. If someone didn't have the right supplies for their home, another person would help them out.

Dad, Maison, Destiny, and I all helped Alex and Aunt Alexandra in rebuilding their house, while Yancy rested to the side. "That was some smart thinking, Stevie!" Alex crowed. "We sure make a great team!"

I knew she meant all of us, including my Earth friends, Maison, Destiny, and Yancy. I cast a look at Dad and didn't say anything.

"Yeah," I said. "You're crazy for adventure, Alex, but when we're in a pinch, you're a great person to have around."

That got her to laugh in delight.

Then Dad, Maison, Destiny, Yancy, and I went to our village to let them know the Wither had been taken care of. I carried Ossie, and we brought the Earth portal with us. The villagers near our home had also taken the time to fix up their village. We brought Yancy back to what was left of our home, where Dad gave him food and milk. By the time he was done eating and drinking, Yancy was good as new.

"What are you going to do about your house, Steve?" Destiny asked Dad once she was convinced Yancy was fine.

"I've built a few smaller houses, so we'll sleep in one of those tonight," Dad said. "Tomorrow, we'll start fixing this up."

"We'll fix up the tree house, too, Stevie," Maison told me. "The next time I visit the Overworld. We'll make it even better than before! I have some new ideas I want to try."

"It's too bad it takes so much longer to make things on Earth," Yancy said. "In *Minecraft* you can work really fast. I'm thinking of those houses that were destroyed by the earthquake."

"I can help," Dad had said.

I stared at Dad. We all stared at Dad. Didn't Dad not like Earth? We had the Earth portal sitting in the room with us, and it gave me an idea.

That night, after the sun set, we went through the portal to Earth, taking Dad with us. We made sure to head out late so that people would be at home and not paying attention if any blocky-looking Overworld citizens were walking the streets. Yancy had something called a "driver's license" and he squeezed all of us into his car and drove us to the houses that needed fixing. Dad thought the car was the most absurd thing he'd ever seen until he saw how fast it could go. Then he was trying to figure out how to make one for himself and was frustrated when Yancy couldn't tell him.

"This is the damage your earthquake has done?" Dad asked as we surveyed the damaged houses.

"Yes. You can see it's a lot," Maison said. "The people who live here are staying in shelters tonight."

"This is easily fixed," said Dad, being the master crafter he was. "You kids keep an eye out for mobs while I take care of this."

Maison and I exchanged amused looks. Dad *still* didn't understand how Earth was different from the Overworld!

Since we didn't really have to keep a lookout for mobs, we all pitched in with Dad, setting the house back up. It was a little confusing for Dad at first since not everything was in a blocked shape, but the people who'd worked on the houses during the day had left their supplies for the night. Within a couple hours, all the houses in the area were fixed and ready to be lived in again.

"I can't wait until morning, when the owners see this!" Maison said excitedly. "I'm sure they'll be so happy!"

"They'll never know who did it, either," Yancy said.

"They don't have to know," Dad said. "What's important is that it's done."

He turned and looked slowly at me. "I think it's time Stevie and I go back through the portal to the Overworld," he said. "I will see all of you again later."

I was a little surprised by his tone. He wasn't rudely telling them to stay away, but he was making it clear he wanted some alone time with me. Was he still trying to do that whole father-son day thing? That had started this morning, though it felt like a million years ago!

"I'll see you guys later!" I told my friends after Yancy had driven us back to Maison's house so we could use her computer as a portal to return. "And hopefully next time we won't have to deal with any more mobs."

Maison smiled. "I think Alex's love of adventure is starting to rub off on me," she said. "If there ever is another mob like Herobrine or the Wither, you know we'll be there for you."

"Yeah," Destiny said. "Our whole lives have changed since we met you, Stevie. We do everything together now."

Even if Dad didn't like me going back and forth between the worlds, I knew my friends understood why I did it. I thought about how I'd first met Maison as a bullied, insecure girl, and Destiny and Yancy as cyberbullies who didn't have any friends and didn't know how to talk to people or channel their anger in helpful ways. Now we were a team that kept saving the Overworld . . . and we were friends. I hoped Dad could see that.

We'd put the Earth portal in the house where Dad and I were staying that night, so that's where we arrived when we jumped through. I knew we wouldn't keep the portal there for long, and I wondered if Dad would help me make a new little house to keep the portal safe in. Ossie was sleeping peacefully near the portal, and when she saw us return, she rolled over and started purring.

"Thanks for coming to Earth with us," I said to Dad, because I felt a need to say something. Other than the purring, there was only silence between Dad and me. It was awkward. "I know you don't like Earth much, but I bet Maison's right about the people whose houses we fixed being really happy."

Dad turned and looked at me in surprise. "I never said I didn't like Earth," he said. "It's just not my home, the same way it's not your home."

"Oh," I said. "I just thought . . ." I trailed off. I didn't entirely know what I'd thought.

Dad shook his head. "Sit down, Stevie."

Uh-oh. Was I in trouble?

Slowly, not taking my eyes away from Dad, I sat down. Dad was looking out at the dark landscape of the Overworld, where we could see zombies and skeletons in the distance. Scary as they were, I knew we were safe in our house. It also felt good to know at least these were normal Overworld mobs, not Nether ones.

"Our father-son day didn't exactly go as planned," Dad was saying. "I wanted us to have a father-son day because recently it feels as if I don't even exist for you."

I was surprised. Was I wrong this whole time when I thought Dad didn't like Earth and my friends? Was Dad just jealous of me going to Earth and seeing Maison, Destiny, and Yancy?

"It's hard seeing your son grow up," Dad said, still not looking at me. "I've tried to teach you what you need to know in the Overworld, and sometimes I've come up short. You still make mistakes. You left that Nether portal, and you never questioned why you saw that Wither."

I cringed. Yes, I was in trouble.

I expected to get lectured on everything I'd done wrong, but then Dad turned and looked at me full in the face. "However, I also see you've learned things I've never taught you," he said. "Your quick thinking helped defeat the Wither, and so did your friends. I'm glad they came along to help us."

Wait, so I wasn't in trouble?

"You said you weren't going to be responsible for them," I said. "Then I saw you nursing Yancy. How come?"

Dad shook his head. "Whenever I've seen you make a mistake, I've corrected you," he said. Boy, that was for sure! "But it's harder for me to own up to my mistakes. It was a mistake for me to think your friends wouldn't help. I think the real reason I've been pushing them away is because it almost seems as if you like them better than me."

It's true! He was jealous!

Dad saw my stunned look and seemed to realize he'd shared something really personal. He cleared his throat and said more seriously, "But finding new friends is also part of growing up. I just want some time with you as well. You've been on so many adventures lately, and I feel as if I've let you down on each one of them. You kept having to save me, when I felt that as a father, I should be the one saving you. But today . . ." He smiled at me. "Today we got to have an adventure together, and when we were alone in the dungeon with that Wither, we were a team. We saved each other. It wasn't the father-son day I was planning, but it was still a very special father-son day."

"Really?" I said. "But the Wither broke your sword! And we have to rebuild our house!"

"The sword and the house don't matter to me," Dad said. "They're both easily fixed. What matters to me is that you're safe. It isn't easy raising a son on your own, but it also isn't easy growing up. You're becoming a young man, Stevie, and I couldn't be more proud of you."

I knew my face was getting red. It felt as if Dad was saying things he'd been wanting to say for a long time and had been unable to. Any time Dad tried to say things that were mushy, he'd stop and get embarrassed before he said much. It sounded as if he were really unloading his soul here.

"I have something for you," I said, reaching into my tool kit. I pulled out the gleaming orb of the Nether star. "I picked it up after I knew that Yancy was okay. I think you should put it to use as a beacon for our new house."

"I have a better idea," Dad said. "When you and Maison rebuild your tree house, you should put it there. That way everyone who goes by will know that a very special group of kids likes to play in that tree house—a group of kids who have saved the Overworld time and again. I just hope I can come along on a few of those future adventures with you."

I laughed. "I don't know," I said. "I think I might need a little break from all these adventures." I paused and thought for a minute. "Hey, Dad?" I said. "How about we make rebuilding the house into another father-son day? I kind of want to remake my bedroom so it's bigger."

"That's not the only thing we should change when we rebuild the house," Dad said. "Until now, we've kept the portal to Earth in that little house nearby to keep it protected from mobs. But why don't we just make a new room in our house and keep it there? It can be the portal room."

My eyes lit up. If the portal was in our own house, that really showed that Dad did take it seriously and did care about my friendships, and Earth! "Yes!" I said. "And maybe when we're done, we can try to make a car like Yancy has. I don't know if it will work, but . . ."

"Stevie," Dad said, "I would love that."

Within a few days Dad's and my house was as all repaired. In fact, it was even better than it had been before.

Dad and I didn't have much success making ourselves a car that worked, but it was still fun. All this time we were spending together was making me feel that even though Dad and I were really different in some ways, that was okay. We each had our strengths and weaknesses, and we complemented each other and helped each other out. We were family, no matter what.

I got to show Maison, Alex, Destiny, and Yancy around our new, big house, including my new, bigger bedroom. They especially oohed and aahed over the new portal room. It was small and simple, but it housed the portal, right under my own roof.

Then we rebuilt the tree house, my friends and I. Dad waited this out, as if he knew some things were best to do with friends, like how some things were best to do with dads. I took the Nether star, added some glass and obsidian that hadn't been destroyed in Dad's supply shed, and created a beacon.

When Dad came out to see the new tree house, he admired how we'd added on to the balconies and put even more furniture in it. When he saw the beacon perched on top of the tree house, he said, "That's the star that will always remind you that you defeated the Wither."

I looked at everyone around me, at Dad, Maison, Alex, Destiny, and Yancy. We'd been through so many things together. I could see that they were all smiling.

"No," I said. "That's the star that will always remind me of how special my family and friends are, because we all came together to make this happen."

The beacon glittered into the sky like a promise we'd always be together.

Check out the rest of the
Unofficial Overworld Adventure series
o find out what happens to Stevie, Alex, and their friends!

Escape from the
Overworld
DANICA DAVIDSON

Attack on the
Overworld
DANICA DAVIDSON

The Rise of
Herobrine
DANICA DAVIDSON

Down into the
Nether
DANICA DAVIDSON

The Armies of
Herobrine
DANICA DAVIDSON

Battle with the
Wither
DANICA DAVIDSON

Available wherever books are sold!

DO YOU LIKE FICTION FOR MINECRAFTERS?

Read the
Unofficial Minecrafters Academy series!

Zombie Invasion
WINTER MORGAN

Skeleton Battle
WINTER MORGAN

Battle in the
Overworld
WINTER MORGAN

DO YOU LIKE FICTION FOR MINECRAFTERS?

Read the Unofficial Minetrapped Adventure series!

Trapped in the Overworld
WINTER MORGAN

Mobs in the Mine
WINTER MORGAN

Terror on a Treasure Hunt
WINTER MORGAN

Ghastly Battle
WINTER MORGAN

Creeper Invasion
WINTER MORGAN

Attack of the Ender Dragon
WINTER MORGAN

DO YOU LIKE FICTION FOR MINECRAFTERS?

You'll Love Books for Terrarians!

Attack of the Goblin Army
Winter Morgan

Snow Fight
Winter Morgan

Welcome to Terraria, a land of adventure and mystery. Build a shelter, craft weapons to battle bosses, explore the biomes, collect coins and gems . . .

Join Miles and his friends on amazing adventures in

The Tales of a Terrarian Warrior series!

Available wherever books are sold!